# Forever

Northern Lights Books for Children are published by
Red Deer Press
A Fitzhenry & Whiteside Company
1512, 1800-4 Street S.W.
Calgary Alberta Canada T2S 2S5
www.reddeerpress.com


**Acknowledgments**

Edited for the Press by Peter Carver
Design by Blair Kerrigan/Glyphics
Printed and bound in Canada by Friesens for Red Deer Press

The author is grateful to Dennis Johnson and Red Deer Press for supporting this project, to master editor Peter Carver, who conceived the book and fine tuned it, and to Edie Van Alstine, whose fine eye and ear are treasured.

Financial support provided by the Canada Council, the Government of Canada through the Book Publishing Industry Development Program (BPIDP), and the Alberta Foundation for the Arts, a beneficiary of the Lottery Fund of the Government of Alberta.

COMMITTED TO THE DEVELOPMENT OF CULTURE AND THE ARTS

THE CANADA COUNCIL | LE CONSEIL DES ARTS
FOR THE ARTS | DU CANADA
SINCE 1957 | DEPUIS 1957

**National Library of Canada Cataloguing in Publication**

MacGregor, Roy, 1948–
Forever : the annual hockey classic / Roy MacGregor ; illustrator, Brian Deines.
ISBN 0-88995-306-6
1. Hockey stories, Canadian (English).  I. Deines, Brian  II. Title.
PS8575.G84F67 2005     jC813'.54     C2005-904195-1

5 4 3 2 1

The illustrations in *Forever* were painted in oil on canvas.

THE ANNUAL HOCKEY CLASSIC

# Forever

ROY MacGREGOR • *Paintings by* BRIAN DEINES

RED DEER PRESS

# THE CHRISTMAS CLASSIC

Forever — we've been doing it *absolutely* forever!" To Bump, it seemed as if he'd been *waiting* forever. Bump's dream — for as long as he could remember dreams that didn't involve being chased through quicksand by green witches — had been to play in the Christmas Classic.

The Christmas Classic had been going on, as Bump's grandpa kept repeating, *"forever."*

The Christmas Classic was really nothing special to someone who might be driving by trying to pry the lid open on a cup of drive-through coffee. It was just a shinny hockey game on a shoveled pond on the outskirts of a little northern town. But to those who played, and those who, like Bump, dreamed of one day playing, the Classic was the highlight of the year.

Bigger than school letting out.

Bigger than birthdays.

Bigger than Halloween.

Bigger, even, *than Christmas itself!*

The Christmas Classic began, Bump had to believe from the way his grandpa talked about it, sometime around the time the last Ice Age wiped out the dinosaurs.

It had been started up — sometime after a long-ago war — by Bump's grandpa, Denzil Finnigan, and "the Uncles." The Uncles being Denzil's five brothers: Eric the goaltender, Brent and Andy the defencemen, and Jimmy and Donny joining Denzil on forward.

"A full roster," Bump's grandpa said from behind the newspaper that fluttered and snapped between the older man and the grandson standing at the foot of the easy chair. "The world's first example of perfect family planning."

And Grandpa roared with laughter as if this had been the first time he had ever *heard* such a thing, let alone said it himself more times than anyone in the sprawling Finnigan family could count.

There was a trophy that went with the Christmas Classic. It was a chrome hubcap that had jumped off a new Chevrolet one hot summer day. The shiny car had somehow missed the turnoff that led out to the four-lane highway that ran south to the big city. It had turned at the Finnigan farm gate, and the flashing chrome hubcap had been the only thing left after a high rooster tail of yellow dust had settled back down on the lane.

The hubcap became the Christmas Classic trophy, and every year since it was taken to the local jeweler's to be engraved with the name of that year's Most Valuable Player.

Jimmy Finnigan MVP 1962, 196?, 1964

Bump's grandpa, a big round man with a bushy mustache you could hide anything in but a smile, took the trophy down from the fireplace mantel and let Bump run his finger over the tiny lettering.

Now that Bump could read, he said the names out loud as his finger traced the years:

*"Denzil Finnigan, MVP, Christmas 1958.*

*". . . Eric Finnigan, MVP, Christmas 1959.*

*". . . Jimmy Finnigan, MVP, Christmas 1962, 1963, 1964 . . . ."*

Bump wondered if his own name would ever grace this treasure. And would they engrave "Bump," the name his grandpa had given him just because he fell down a lot when he was learning to walk? Or would it be "Walter," the name only his grade three teacher, Mrs. Whipsnide, used for him?

No one else ever called him anything but "Bump," and there were times when he wondered if he would carry the nickname for the rest of his life — eventually turning into a man much like his father, heading off to work carrying a briefcase and called "Bump" by his clients.

Much more alarming, of course, was that they might actually call him "Walter."

It didn't really matter, so long as one day his name joined those on the trophy that seemed to stretch back . . . forever.

And, of course, so long as he beat Poodle there.

Bump's older sister, Annie — nicknamed "Poodle" by their grandpa on account of her thick head of curling, black hair — was already playing in the Classic.

Two winters ago, Poodle had come down to the cleared-off pond, wearing a sandwich board her mother and Grandma had helped her paint, and picketed the Christmas Classic. The older women had watched from the bay window as Poodle had marched round and round the little rink until, finally, Grandpa had skated over and handed her a stick.

An official invitation to join in.

Poodle had already played a season of ringette and was now playing organized hockey in town. She said she'd probably be playing in the Olympics before Bump would ever be asked to play in the Christmas Classic.

And though Bump knew it was just Poodle teasing — she delivered this announcement with a loud raspberry, a stuck-out tongue, and a handful of loose snow down the back of Bump's shirt — he worried that she just might turn out to be right.

It seemed as though everyone else in the world was now allowed in. Poodle's picketing had opened up the Classic to other young women. And now there were great uncles and younger uncles and aunts and nieces and nephews all playing the game.

There was even a dog, Grandpa's old fat Lab — "Puck" — who was always welcome to play. Though now he had grown so lazy he barely flicked a soft black ear when someone in the game shouted "Puck!" for reasons that had absolutely nothing to do with the fat old dog lying on the ridge of the nearest snowbank.

"Be patient," Grandpa told Bump.

"Patience," his father said.

"You're too small," Poodle said, down a twitching nose at her little brother. "You'd probably fall down the drinking hole."

Bump loved, and feared, the drinking hole. While the Uncles scraped the ice clear for the game, Grandpa cut out the hole with his ice-fishing auger, a tall, blue piece of equipment that looked like a giant's drill.

Grandpa leaned into the large tool and twisted the handle until the blades bit into the ice, his shoulder pressing down and his hand turning while the auger churned up white ice and then, magically, broke through and plunged deep into the pond.

Grandpa caught the handle and lifted, water pouring up as the auger popped back out and then, suddenly, what had been white shavings around blue ice became a black, alarming hole.

Bump marveled over how dark and menacing the water could look in winter when it seemed so clear and inviting in summer when they swam here.

No one ever drank from the pond in summer. In winter, all the players did.

Bump knew from the way the Uncles gasped and licked their lips that the water must taste different to those who played than to those who did not.

To Bump, it always seemed he was drinking something that the smallmouth bass and snapping turtles and leeches were swimming around in.

As for the Uncles, it always seemed to Bump as if they were drinking something that, if anyone ever figured out how to bottle it, would put Pepsi and Coca-Cola out of business before spring arrived.

Bump wanted to taste the drinking-hole water the way it tasted to the players.

More than anything else in the world, more than any Christmas present he could ever imagine asking for, he wanted to play in the Classic.

"One day soon," his father said.

"Never, little boy," Poodle said.

"Your time will come," Grandpa said.

"Okay," Bump said in a small, unsure voice.

It would happen — sometime.

But if forever took any longer, Bump thought, he wouldn't be able to stand it.

# MEASURING UP

Every Christmas Eve, Grandma — a short, thick woman with hair so white and soft it seemed her head was wrapped in its own private cloud — measured Bump up. "Let's see where you stand, my Bump," she said as she twisted a long yellow HB school pencil into a small sharpener she had taken from the top kitchen drawer. "I was just saying to your mother that you look like you've shot up this past year."

With Bump's hopes soaring, Grandma carefully pulled across the sliding door that separated her big airy kitchen from the dining room.

Bump had to stand against the sliding door while Grandma pushed down on his shoulder so he couldn't lift his heels and cheat. Then, using the long yellow pencil held level across the very tip of his head, she drew a line on the door to show where he stood at that precise moment in his life.

It was an annual event, and Grandma did it with all the grandchildren, carefully recording names and dates beside each mark.

Each of the grandchildren then turned, anxious to check how he or she measured up to the dozens of other dated marks on Grandma's door — not to mention how they measured up to themselves as they had been exactly one year ago this day.

Last year, Bump had barely reached the same level Uncle Donny had been on Christmas Eve 1952.

But this year it seemed he *towered* over the Christmas Eve 1952 version of Uncle Donny.

"*My,*" said Grandma, "would you look at that? You *have* shot up!"

Bump turned and stood so close to the sliding door that the lines and scribbles seemed blurred, but he could still trace Grandma's finger from his own fresh mark to one of great significance from the distant past. He had finally caught his dad's mark from Christmas Eve 1968.

While the others oohed and ahhhed over Bump's now provable "growth spurt," he raced upstairs to check the only proof he required to gain admission to the Christmas Classic.

*Was his dad in the 1968 photo?*

The photographs held the history of the Christmas Classic.

The photographs were framed and lined the upstairs hallway in his grandparents' old two-story farmhouse on the sugarbush hill overlooking the pond.

They were hanging in order, each year counted off by a single snapshot — the early ones black and white, the later ones full color — of the sweating, sagging, smiling players at the end of the annual game.

Bump had been studying the framed pictures for as long as he could remember.

Perhaps even longer — because, of course, he wouldn't remember.

He could see his grandpa's big mustache change from black to white as the snapshots changed from black and white to color.

He could watch the Uncles change, hair thinning and waists thickening as if all five of them were outfitted with those little rubber air valves that car tires have — and a little more air was being pumped in after each Classic.

What never changed were the grins — big, wide, mischievous, Finnigan grins that were as common in this family as big feet and bad tempers might be in another.

Bump often began at the first picture along the wall to show Puck sitting in front of the players. Between the doorway to his grandparents' bedroom and the door to the washroom, he could trace Puck's growth from puppy to frisky young dog to the fat old dog he now was.

Bump loved the stories of a young Puck running off with the real pucks. Grandma would later find them buried in her garden. And Bump wondered how old Puck, who could barely bother waddling down the lane to watch the game these days, could once have been considered, as Grandpa often said with a wild bellow, *"The toughest defenceman to get around the Christmas Classic has ever known!"*

The framed photographs now ran virtually the entire length of the wallpapered hallway.

Sometimes there was snow; sometimes there was none. In one, the snow was blowing so hard it was difficult to make out the individual players.

In another, there was no snow — but the pond was frozen solid and the players all bundled up as if they expected the blizzard to blow in from the next picture frame over.

Bump could watch his own father, Wilf, spring up as if someone had pinched his head and pulled him up as though he was made of plasticine.

The Uncles, on the other hand, looked as if someone else had placed a thumb on their heads and pushed down, their plasticine spreading, the thumb rubbing off their once bushy hair.

But the black-and-white snapshot Bump was most interested at this moment was the first one that Wilf Finnigan had appeared in. Before he had stretched like plasticine. Before he was ever named MVP of the Christmas Classic.

The very *first* picture of Bump's father as a player.

If his dad *was* in the photograph of the 1968 Classic — and if Bump today and his dad in 1968 were, as the door said, exactly the same size — then surely this would be the year Bump would finally be allowed to play.

His heart pounded as he searched for the framed photograph, then sank as he found it.

*There was no sign of his dad in the picture.*

Bump checked 1969.

And there, standing in the front row, his smile as big and bright as the chrome hubcap in the big hands of Uncle Jimmy, once again that year's MVP, was his dad, Wilf Finnigan.

Bump would have to wait another year — and he would have to hope he grew as much, in that one year, as his dad had grown between Christmas 1968 and Christmas 1969.

"Some people never grow," Poodle told him when they were shaking presents under the tree that evening. "They just stop like *that*" — she snapped her fingers — "and never grow another speck. Grandma told me it runs in our family."

Bump didn't believe her. Where, then, was the tiny uncle who had never been allowed to play? But he still didn't like what she said. For the rest of the evening, he felt as if someone had squeezed an onion in his eyes.

Maybe, he thought, they will ask me this year anyway. Why not? People were doing everything younger these days — so why not playing in the Christmas Classic?

He let his hopes soar when Grandpa took him down to the frozen pond earlier in the morning and gave him a short skating lesson.

It wasn't as if Bump couldn't skate — he'd been in hockey programs for almost as long as he'd been in school. But Grandpa said Bump needed work on his turns and was going to show him how to do them more smoothly.

Bump's method of turning was to "snowplow" to slow down and then turn abruptly. Grandpa's method was to skate even harder, to move one leg over the other and dig in, pushing off as hard as possible as he came out of the turn.

Grandpa demonstrated his own turns — big, powerful, looping turns — to Bump and then cupped his big hands under Bump's arms and all but carried him through a long series of turns.

Bump could feel his Grandpa's skating power as if it were his own. He could feel the wind Grandpa's speed created as it blew the hair that hung out from under his toque. He found himself screaming at times, in delight and terror.

Bump figured this skating lesson was merely a practice run for the big moment.

# DOWN THE HOLE

When the Classic got under way, he carried his little skates and his little sawed-off road hockey stick down to the pond in the hopes that they would, finally, ask him to play. But they didn't.

"Don't fall down the drinking hole," Poodle warned, giggling into the shoulder of her latest ridiculous boyfriend as the two skated off from where Bump stood.

"Keep your head up," Dad told him, though Bump wasn't exactly sure if he meant during the game or if he should happen to fall down the drinking hole.

Bump stood, shivering and feeling sorry for himself, as his grandpa, his dad, the Uncles, the younger uncles, two aunts, his sister and her boyfriend, several girl cousins, and a dozen or more boy cousins got ready for the Classic.

The Uncles had already hauled out the nets: two contraptions, one at each end, both made of plastic plumbing pipes fitted together and glued by Grandpa up in the work shed. The pipes had then been covered with burlap sacking Grandma had sewn together in a fit as perfect as the throws she made for the old living room furniture. They hauled out plywood boards from the barn. They took the boards and rammed them hard into the snowbanks back of each net. This, they hoped, would prevent pucks from flying down the ice and getting lost in the bulrushes in the swampy ends of the pond.

They then chose up sides, everyone throwing his or her stick into a wild pile at center ice. Uncle Jimmy, his eyes pinched ridiculously tight to show they were closed, then crawled on his hands and knees to the pile and began tossing them, one by one, to one side or the other of center. The rule was that players then simply followed their sticks to find out which side they were on.

"You're peeking," Uncle Eric called out.

"Cheater!'" Uncle Brent shouted.

"Am not!" Uncle Jimmy cried, sitting up and squeezing his eyes even tighter, as if this somehow proved to everyone that he was dividing up the teams fairly.

Bump's grandpa, in his biggest voice, went over the rules, just as he had the year before — and had, likely, since the Ice Age killed off the dinosaurs and the Christmas Classic had started up.

*"Two games, first to 10 wins. If we split, we play a rubber. No slashing. No raisees. No golf shots. No hip checks."*

And with that, Grandpa turned and stared, hard and determined, at Uncle Jimmy, who put on his best choirboy look and nodded back while everyone else laughed. Sure as there would be a third game to break a tie, sure as no one was supposed to slash or hoist a puck into those parts of the body that fear even foam pucks, Uncle Jimmy could be counted on at some point to come flying across the ice with his butt sticking out like a runaway Zamboni. And just as certain, the chosen player— each year a different one — would go spilling over the snowbanks screaming for a penalty that was never called.

How could it be? No rules had ever been set up for penalties. Everyone was just expected to behave properly. Even Uncle Jimmy — with the singular exception of the one hip check he was permitted each Christmas Classic.

Bump's grandpa slammed his stick down hard on the ice several times. Bump noticed that the old man's stick, unlike all the others, had no curve to it. He wondered how Grandpa could even shoot. Once Denzil Finnigan had everyone's attention, he made his annual announcement.

"*Laaaaadiessss and gennnulmennnn,*" he said in his biggest voice, "*the national anthem.*"

They stood at attention, all the players on the ice, little Bump on the snowbank, some with hats off, some on, some with their hands over their hearts, some with their arms ramrod straight down by their side.

And together, in on-key and off-key voices, in baritones, and sopranos, and altos, and in the little squeaks that came from the little boy on the snowbank, they sang "O Canada."

Some shuffled on their skates the way National Hockey League players do when they're on the ice for the anthem. Some swayed back and forth to the music the way NHL players on the bench do. Some, like Denzil Finnigan, never moved an inch.

The anthem done, Grandpa dropped the puck.

Uncle Jimmy won it by plucking the puck out of the air before it struck the ice.

"*Illegal!*" Uncle Donny yelled, but even Uncle Donny was laughing as Uncle Jimmy spun back and circled to begin the first rush up the fresh ice surface.

The Christmas Classic was on.

Bump stood in the same "at attention" stance he had maintained through the anthem. And then his shoulders slumped. He stood, watching and listening to the crack of stick on puck, the thud of puck against the backboards, the sizzle and scrape of skate blades in the corners, the whoops and shouts of the players . . .

And then, sometime around the point where the game was tied 7-7, Bump felt his right foot break through the crust on the bank. Down, down, down, down he plummeted — until he was, instantly, stuck fast and screaming at the top of his lungs for help.

"*HELLPPPPP!*"

Finally, they noticed him.

To the players stopping to see what the screaming was all about, it must have looked as if Bump had lost his head up in the big house and it had rolled out the front door, down the hill and along the laneway and somehow bounced up onto the snowbank at the side of the rink. And here it had magically settled, toque up and face forward, tears pouring out of the eyes and screams out of the mouth.

"*HHHHHELLLLPPPPPPPPP MMMEEE!*"

Bump was terrified the ice might give way a second time on him, and down he would plummet into a dark, black "drinking hole" filled with snapping turtles and leeches desperately hungry from their long winter stuck in the mud.

*"HHHHELLPPPPPPPPPP!"*

They suspended the game while the Uncles, working carefully with the big scrapers and the blades of their hockey sticks, extricated poor Bump. The rest of the players leaned on their sticks and watched, most of them — but certainly not Poodle — trying not to laugh too loudly at the boy stuck in the snowbank.

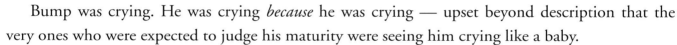

Two of the Uncles yanked up at once and Bump popped out of the snowbank like a wine cork at the end of a corkscrew.

The head, it turned out, had a body.

Only the body was minus one boot.

And a wet, woolen, gray sock was dangling off the freezing toes of the bootless foot.

Bump was crying. He was crying *because* he was crying — upset beyond description that the very ones who were expected to judge his maturity were seeing him crying like a baby.

The more he tried to stop, the more he cried because he could not stop.

"Quit it, you big baby," Poodle told him, a grin like an illegal curve on her face. "I mean, 'you *little* baby!'"

Bump began to sob. He began to sob and shake and Uncle Donny, presuming it was the cold making Bump shake, picked him up as if he were little more than a toddler.

Holding Bump close to his chest, Uncle Donny skated across the ice and climbed the snowbank with his skates still on and handed Bump off — *like a baby* — to Bump's mother who had come down to see what all the commotion was about.

The other Uncles were still trying to retrieve the lost boot. They dug with the scrapers and poked their hockey sticks down the hole like dentists working on a huge cavity, but their prodding and picking and plucking produced nothing.

"Don't worry about it," Bump's grandpa told them. "It'll bubble up in the spring. I'll have it for him by next winter."

Bump could hear them laughing behind him.

He never wanted to see that boot again.

Never.

# TOO BIG

But Bump was not to have his wish.

He forgot all about the boot.

He came to his grandparents' farm a dozen times before the first snowfall of the next winter, but Grandpa never mentioned the lost boot.

Maybe it had sunk so deep into the mud it would never be found.

Spring came and the pond came to life, small peepers making the farmhouse sound at night as if a doorbell were constantly ringing.

Summer came and the air filled with dragonflies, their abandoned waterbug bodies left like open suitcases on the rocks around the pond.

Fall came and the pond coated with fallen leaves: bright red and orange from the maple; dark red from the thick oak at the end of the laneway.

At Thanksgiving, when the grandparents held their other big dinner of the year, the kids awoke to find a layer of ice as thin and clear as window pane on the pond, and they spent the morning shattering the glass with small stones.

In the late afternoon, it began to snow.

And when the snow came down, the boot came out.

"Bump," Grandpa said at the end of the turkey dinner when the Uncles had already fallen asleep sitting in front of the television with a football game shouting at them. "I almost forgot — I found this sometime back in April."

He pulled his hand from behind his back.

It was the boot.

It was blue.

"Baby color," Poodle said.

It was small.

"Baby size," Poodle said.

Grandpa looked at the little boot, shook it as if expecting spiders to spill from it, and then looked hard at Bump's foot.

"I'm not so sure this is going to fit," Grandpa said, his big mustache dipping down in a frown.

With Bump a reluctant participant, Grandpa got down and pulled Bump's foot up from the side of the chair.

He put the blue boot over Bump's toes and began sliding it on.

Bump was horrified.

He felt as if he couldn't even dress himself!

He felt like a . . . *baby!*

But then the boot stuck.

His grandpa pushed hard.

It stuck fast.

His grandpa wiggled hard and pushed harder.

But nothing.

His grandpa looked up, the mustache flipping into a smile.

"This boot's for *babies*," he said. "You've grown too much."

Bump felt his skin shiver, but it was a shiver quite unlike the one that had rippled like a flag down his spine that previous winter when they had popped him out of the snowbank.

*He was growing!*

*He was too big for the boot!*

But was he big enough for the Christmas Classic?

He looked at his grandpa, who was grinning in his eyes as well as his mustache.

He looked at Poodle, her mouth once again an illegal curve — but this time turned upside down.

He smiled at her.

# TALKING ICE, TALKING SANTA

Soon after school let out for the Christmas holidays, the Finnigan family gathered once again at the old farmhouse for the traditional Christmas Eve dinner and, of course, the traditional Christmas Day Classic.

There was a difference this time, though. The grandparents had run out of space with all the new boyfriends, new girlfriends, new husbands, new wives, and new baby Finnigans that were now showing up each year. Most still slept at the big farmhouse, but others stayed in town with various Uncles and aunts.

Bump's family brought snowshoes and toboggans up from the city and, with old Puck coming along with them, they hauled sleeping bags and groceries out to the lake nearby where the Finnigans had kept a small fishing cabin for as long as Bump's own father could remember.

The cabin wasn't much: simple, square, and smelling of cedar — and, in the dead of winter, a bit musty.

It was colder inside than out when they arrived, but while Bump and Poodle rode toboggans down the hill and out onto the ice, the parents built a good fire in the stone fireplace. By dark, the little cabin was as cozy as the big farmhouse.

It was getting late and Bump crossed his fingers — perhaps later he'd even cross his legs — in hopes that he wouldn't need to make the long trek up the shoveled path to the ice-cold outhouse.

But his father insisted he go anyway, even if Bump argued he didn't have to. They went up together, their feet stuffed into their big winter boots. But they wore no winter jackets, toques, or mittens as they hurried along the path and did what needed to be done.

Bump wanted to hurry down as quickly as he'd run up the hill, but his father held him back with nothing but a finger to his lips that they should be as silent as possible.

Bump stood, shaking, less from the cold than the sense of awe.

He followed his father's stare up, straight up into a night sky so clear and bright it seemed somehow to have been strung from one end to the other with white Christmas lights.

It was as if the sky were no longer a dome, but had depth. Some of the stars felt so bright and close it seemed they should have chain strings hanging from them for turning off and on.

"There's the Milky Way," Bump's dad said, pointing to the one cloudy area of the night sky.

"How many stars are there in it?" Bump asked.

"No one knows," his dad answered. "The universe goes on . . . *forever*.."

Just like the Christmas Classic, Bump thought. Just like my waiting to play. But before he could say anything, something rumbled in the distance, a low growl like someone's stomach or an African lion.

"The ice is talking," Bump's father said.

"Ice can't talk."

"It talks when it's shifting," Bump's father said. "You can hear it all through the night. Sometimes it cracks like a rifle shot when it's really hard. That's the best ice. *Hockey* ice."

In the morning, it was time to head back to the farmhouse, where already the preparations were under way.

Bump's grandma, several of the aunts, and cousin Rodney — who had trained as a chef — were planning and preparing the big meal.

Rodney might have had the qualifications, but Grandma Finnigan was clearly the one in charge.

The turkey was on, the smell of its slow roasting filling the big house all day long like background music.

There were green salads and gelatin salads and coleslaw, deviled eggs, raw vegetables and garlic dip, scalloped potatoes, cranberries, steamed vegetables, chutney, dill pickles, delicious stuffing, despicable asparagus tips, and dreadful broccoli.

There was, of course, Grandma Finnigan's specialty — steaming blueberry pies from her secret berry patch back of the sugarbush hill.

This year, like last year, cousins Tom and Stephanie had their own vegetarian dishes. Bump wondered if the Uncles would once again kid the two of them by growling like wild hyenas while biting into thick turkey drumsticks.

Probably. Some traditions took only a year to start.

Bump's job, also a new tradition, was to carry Grandpa's wine glass to the kitchen and fill it from the big wine bottle Uncle Jimmy always set out.

One of Grandma Finnigan's many jobs was to make sure the wine glass was half filled with water.

Another of her jobs involved her thumbnail.

Hanging once again on the wall of Grandma Finnigan's big kitchen was her beloved Talking Santa.

It was something Bump had never seen in another house.

The Talking Santa was sort of ugly: a hard, plastic Santa face with an open mouth and a long, red, plastic tongue that looked more like a lizard tail hanging down halfway to the linoleum floor.

It had entranced Bump since he was barely a toddler. He had watched, hypnotized, as his Grandma had pulled the long Santa tongue out straight, placed her thumbnail on it, and yanked down hard, Santa's voice filling the kitchen with the strangest sound Bump had ever heard before or since.

*"Merrrrr—rrrrry Churrrissssss-musssss!"*

When he was younger, he had accepted this speech as pure magic, but for some time now Bump had wondered how it was that Grandma's thumbnail could produce such a sound.

A thumb had no voice, and yet when Grandma grabbed the long tongue and yanked, Santa *talked*!

How could that be?

Grandpa showed Bump and Poodle the secret. He held out the tongue and asked them to feel its back. It was rough, grooved — "serrated," Grandpa called it — and felt almost as if someone had nicked the round red plastic cord hundreds of times with a sharp knife.

He took the two youngsters into the living room — Grandpa always called it the "sitting room" — and opened up the old Victrola that the Uncles sometimes cranked up and played scratchy old Elvis Presley records on.

Grandpa cranked the handle and let Bump and Poodle watch closely as he laid the arm and needle onto the groove of a record and the room suddenly filled with an old Elvis song.

*"Ah well, I bless my soul, what's wrong with me . . . "*

Grandpa lifted the needle, one of the Uncles bellowing out a protest from behind the sports pages, and then showed the kids that the old record had little grooves and bumps so small in those grooves that only the needle could pick them up.

"It's the same idea," he said. "Think of Santa's tongue as a record and your thumbnail as the needle."

And to prove his point, he took them back out into the kitchen and demonstrated again and again how the speed of his thumbnail on the back of the cord could make Santa talk fast or slow, growl like a lion or screech like a blue jay.

*"Merrrrr—rrrrry Churrrisssssss-mussssss!"*

*"Mrry Cris-mus!"*

*"Merrrrrrrrrrrrrrrrry Churrrrrrrrrrrrrisssssssssumussssss!"*

*"Merchrsms!"*

*"Merrrrr—rrrrry Churrrisssssss-mussssss!"*

Grandpa had noticed that Grandma was deep in the pantry. She was making a lot of noise, muttering to herself as she searched for a jar of preserves. He used the opportunity to slip quickly over to the counter to pour a fresh glass of wine, leaving Bump and Poodle to try the tongue for themselves.

Poodle could do it, a weak and choppy *"Merr—ry Chrrisssss-mussssss!"* squeaking through the room.

Bump could not. His thumbnails were soft and bent too easily, picking up nothing but a hiss when he pulled down the cord.

"You're too little," Poodle said. "Besides, you chew your nails."

*"Do not!"* Bump hissed.

He sounded like a Talking Santa himself, a *weak* one.

Poodle just turned away, nose high in the air.

She knew she had him.

He knew she had him.

He looked at his poor beaten nails and vowed never again to bite them or suck on them when he had trouble getting to sleep.

# A NEW PLAYER

Grandpa Finnigan always insisted on being served the turkey gizzard.

Bump had no idea what the gizzard was. Some organ, apparently, that only birds had. But he had a good idea what gizzard tasted like: *hideous*. He'd tried a small slice one year and almost gagged while his grandpa laughed so hard his big white mustache bounced like gull wings.

"Eat gizzard," Grandpa announced each year, "and live forever."

So far, nothing had proved him wrong.

Grandpa ate the gizzard, sneaked more glasses of wine, and let his endlessly smiling mustache answer Grandma's endless warnings about his heart and what the doctor had said about too much wine. They ate, popped crackers, wore silly crepe paper hats, read bad jokes, and made silly toasts to one another, as well as to the year just past and the new year to come. And always, as the blueberry pies headed toward second helpings and the tea and coffee pots arrived from the kitchen, the talk turned to hockey.

Well, not exactly "talk." More like *debate*.

"There was no one like the Rocket," Grandpa said in his big voice.

Grandpa had, in his day, been the town's best player and had once gone off to the fall training camp of the Toronto Maple Leafs where he had played in a single exhibition game before being sent home. The match had been against the Montreal Canadiens, when Maurice "Rocket" Richard was at the top of his game.

"I never saw eyes like that in my life. You'd swear he shot with *them*, not his stick."

"Orr for me," Bump's dad countered. "Orr was the greatest ever. No one ever changed the game the way Bobby Orr did."

Bump's dad was smaller than Bump's Grandpa, but very muscular. Wilf Finnigan's head didn't fit with his body. Sort of like a bottle on which someone had screwed the wrong cap. He wore glasses and he was balding — but once you got to the neck he bulged out as if he were, in fact, someone quite different.

Wilf Finnigan even had a tattoo on each of his powerful arms. On the right arm was the Tasmanian Devil cartoon character, "Taz," holding a hockey stick. On the left arm was a heart with the word "Jan" on it.

Bump's dad always said that the tattoo artist had made a spelling mistake.

Bump's mother, Jean, didn't care to talk about it at all.

When it came to Bobby Orr, Bump's dad was speaking from personal knowledge. It was not, however, quite so glorious a personal experience as an actual NHL tryout.

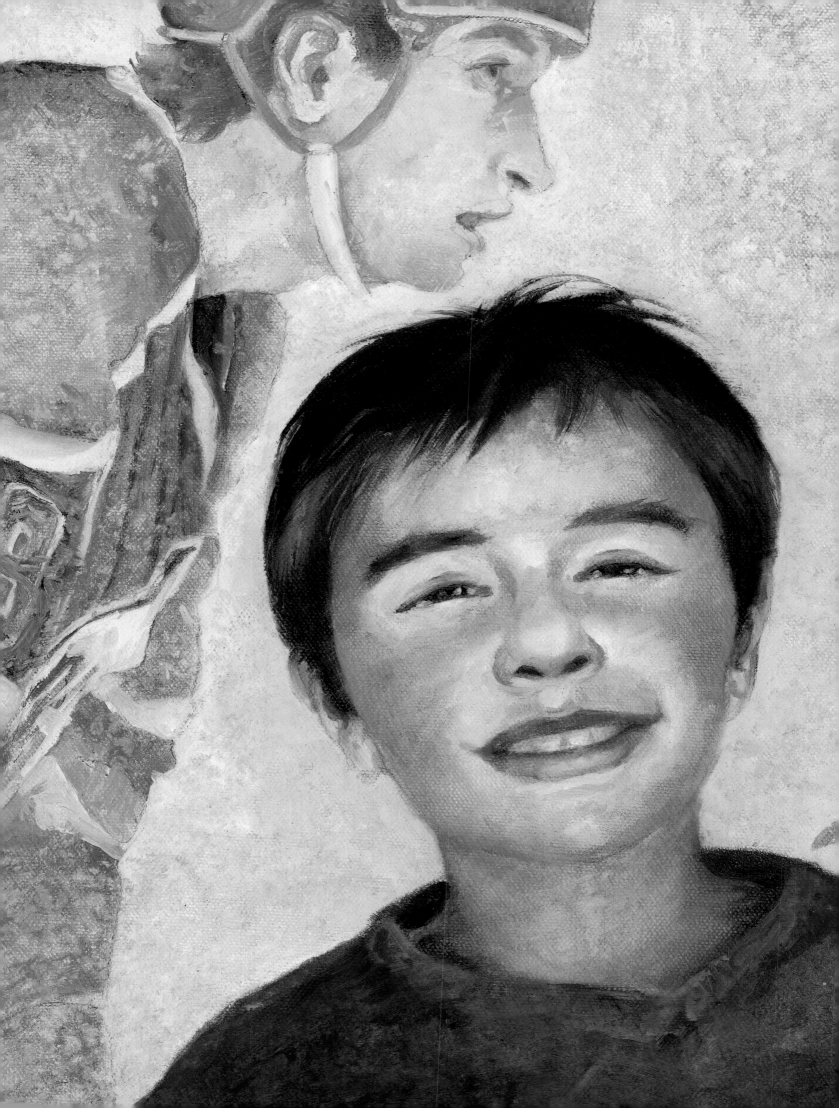

Bump's dad had been a town all-star and Bobby Orr had been the star of the next town over. They had played against each other for years — but always as young children. When Bobby Orr had headed off at age fourteen to play for the Oshawa Generals junior hockey club, Wilf Finnigan had stayed home to play midget and juvenile and a year of intermediate before retiring from competitive hockey.

"Eight years old," Bump's dad said, his fist making the dessert dishes dance as it slammed lightly onto the table, "and he could score from the blueline by shooting the puck *right over* our goalie's head!"

"This young Gretzky," one of the Uncles muttered, shaking his head in awe. "He just might turn out to be the best of all time. I know Orr changed the game for defencemen, but look at what this guy's doing for forwards. Who ever thought about attacking from *behind* the net! Gordie Howe says if they parted this kid's hair at the back they'd probably find a *third eye!*"

And the mere mention of Howe started another of the Uncles off on "The Best of All Time."

Bump sat through the never-ending debate as he had the year before and the year before that. He wasn't thinking about who was best, but whether one day his own name might be mentioned with the likes of Richard and Orr and Gretzky and Howe.

But would he be known as "Bump" or "Walter"?

Neither sounded much like a hockey hero.

As the debate sounded on, Bump tuned out and lost himself in his own dreams. He scored the overtime goal in Game Seven of the Stanley Cup final. He skated around the rink with the cup over his head. He signed a thousand autographs . . .

Bump came back to earth at the scraping sound of a chair being pushed back.

His grandpa was on his feet, a little unsteadily.

Perhaps Grandma hadn't managed as much water in Grandpa's wine as she'd hoped.

"Tomorrow," Grandpa said grandly, raising his wine glass in one final dinner toast, "the Christmas Classic welcomes a new player."

Everyone turned to look at Bump.

Bump figured so much blood was racing to his face he would either burn up or explode.

It was what he'd been waiting to hear . . . forever.

He was being invited to play in the Christmas Classic!

# PART OF THE CLASSIC

Bump hardly slept that night in the little cabin by the lake. It had nothing to do with the strange noises coming from outside — the snapping and popping of a night when the fluid all but vanishes from a thermometer — and everything to do with the Christmas Classic.

He was going to play!

But *how* would he play? Would he humiliate himself like the day he'd lost his boot? Or would he play as he always had in his dreams?

> *Bump, first on the ice, his sharp skates writing the story of his speed on the clean sheet behind him.*
>
> *His skates sizzling like bacon in Grandma's frying pan as he took his first corner.*
>
> *The puck dancing on the blade of his stick as if it were attached by a rubber band.*
>
> *His moves so quick, so fluid, so mysterious that it would be as if he had secret tunnels built through the opposing team.*
>
> *The puck nicking in off the crossbar, the rink exploding in cheers that refused to die down until he had been knocked unconscious by the backslapping of his grateful teammates . . .*

Still, Bump must have slept some, for he awoke to find his dad's hand on his shoulder, lightly shaking him. His father bent down, pressed his cheek to Bump's, and rubbed quickly.

*"No whisker burns!"* Bump yelled.

"Just checking to see if you have any of your own," his dad chuckled. "You're a man today. You're playing in the Classic."

Bump knew there was no way he could have magically sprouted whiskers overnight, but he did feel somehow . . . *bigger* today.

As if waiting forever had become suddenly worth it all.

The Finnigans gathered together at the old farmhouse, exchanged presents, ate, and then, precisely at noon, Grandpa and the Uncles dressed warmly. They pulled their old hockey sweaters over their heads and picked up their skates and sticks and gloves from the front shed. And then they headed down toward the pond.

"You put on a winter coat," Grandma scolded Grandpa. "You'll catch your death."

But Grandpa never even answered. He turned, seemed to wave with his mustache, grinned a little wider, and blew a kiss back at her that seemed to hang in the air like a puff of smoke before he was gone.

The rink was in perfect shape, glistening with anticipation. It would have been shoveled and flooded during the night by Grandpa and the Uncles.

It was cold enough to freeze your nostrils solid when you tried to breathe, so Bump decided to skip his nose and let his mouth hang open, shipping directly to his lungs.

Grandpa called out the familiar rules:

*"Two games, first to 10 wins. If we split, we play a rubber. No slashing. No raisees. No golf shots. No hip checks."*

He stared hard at Uncle Jimmy. Uncle Jimmy looked innocent and puzzled at the same time. Grandpa shook his head, giving up.

*"Laaaaadiesssss and gennnulmennnn,"* Grandpa announced in his biggest voice, *"the national anthem."*

For the first time, Bump was on skates for the anthem. He shuffled his feet back and forth like some of the Uncles. He swayed back and forth like some of his cousins. He stood rock still like his Grandpa. He sang in a voice with less squeak and he knew a few more words of the national anthem than he had a year ago. By next year, he promised himself, he would know it all.

They played and it was everything that Bump had imagined and more. He played neither as badly as he feared nor as grandly as he wished. But he at least fit in. And soon he lost all thought on whether he would make a fool of himself. It was too much fun for fretting.

He loved the noise. He loved the sounds of skates scraping on ice. He loved the hollow knock of the puck against boards. He loved the way, when players shouted, the words seemed to explode from mouths in small bursts of steam.

Sometime nearing the end of the opening match, Bump's dad sent him a cross-ice pass that he caught perfectly on the blade of his stick. Bump began moving up the ice — fast.

*I'm carrying the puck!* he thought to himself. *I'm carrying the puck in the Christmas Classic.*

He never saw Uncle Jimmy's hip coming.

He did, however, see the snowbank coming. Straight at him.

No, *he at it* — Bump leaving the winter pond like a duck taking off in summer, Bump rising into the air and looping high over the ridge of the snowbank and rolling down the far side into a deep drift of fresh snow. He went in headfirst, his toque ripping off from the force.

He instantly panicked — *Oh no, not again!* He couldn't possibly handle the shame of another lost winter garment.

Bump stabbed his hands into the drift in search and felt the lost toque on his first grab.

He looked up.

Every player in the Classic was standing staring down at him, their heads seeming to sit along the snowbank like the blue China plates on the wall of Grandma's big kitchen, and all of them were laughing.

"You're part of the Classic now, son," Bump's dad shouted. "Uncle Jimmy's hip just *officially* initiated you!"

And with that everyone — Bump included — laughed all the harder.

Bump couldn't even feel the pain in his side where Uncle Jimmy's hip check had caught him.

He had, he figured, never felt so good in his life.

He was now part of something that had gone on . . . forever.

# STICK ON THE ICE!

They split the first two matches and had to play a rubber. The Uncles and some of the older cousins quickly scraped the ice clean and they were ready to go one more time.

In the rubber match, with the score tied 9-9 according to Uncle Jimmy's running play-by-play commentary, Bump's grandpa picked up the puck behind his net and began stickhandling up ice.

Grandpa moved steadily, not fast like the younger men, but smoothly and smartly, easily keeping the puck away from checkers.

Bump scrambled to keep up. Once he saw his grandpa look over and see him, the big mustache — now frozen solid, with a white coating of ice — bending slightly as the old man grinned.

*"Go with me!"* he barked from beneath the mustache.

*"And keep your stick on the ice!"*

As Grandpa came into the other side's half, he let the puck drop back off his stick and into his skates.

He never broke stride. One skate blade kicked the puck perfectly over to the other skate blade. The last checkers jabbed helplessly at the puck, their sticks bouncing off the wall formed by Grandpa's two skates. In an instant he was through them and free. His next stride smartly clicked the puck back up onto his stick blade.

Grandpa looked over at Bump and grinned again through his igloo mustache.

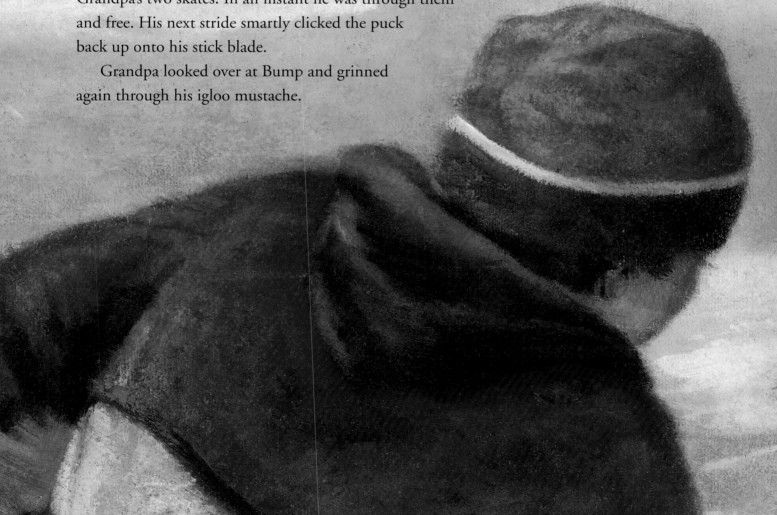

Grandpa and Bump were now all alone on the goaltender, Uncle Eric.

Grandpa dipped a shoulder, leaned as if to fire the puck into the far side, then tucked it back to his backhand.

Uncle Eric guessed, falling toward the backhand shot.

But Grandpa didn't shoot. He pulled the puck back and sent a very soft, painfully slow pass across to Bump.

*Keep your stick on the ice!* Bump told himself. Keep your stick on the ice!

Bump swung with all his might, spilling down as he shot.

All he heard were the cheers as he slid, on his back, right past the net and up onto the snowbank. Almost exactly where, on another Christmas Classic day, he had lost his boot and suffered his greatest humiliation.

The winning team set on him like jackals. They pounded him. They tickled him. They yanked his toque down over his eyes. They pulled him so hard to his feet that he left them and was, momentarily, skating in air.

Uncle Jimmy and Uncle Donny swung him onto their shoulders and began skating around with Bump as if *he* were the Stanley Cup.

*Bump was the hero of the Christmas Classic!*

Uncle Donny had his camera out. He was already organizing the sweating, happy crowd of Finnigans and boyfriends and girlfriends for the group photograph that ended every Classic and would go up on the farmhouse wall.

Bump was placed right up front. He stood directly in front of Uncle Jimmy, who had, once again, been awarded — more accurately, had awarded *himself* — the chrome hubcap as the MVP of the game.

They all squished together. Uncle Donny called out instructions as he framed the shot, then pushed the timer that would give him just enough time to fit himself into the picture before the flash went off.

Bump felt a big hand on his shoulder.

It was Grandpa, leaning down, his ice mustache dripping smiles.

"A goal like that," Grandpa said, "you'll remember forever."

# CHANGES

And Bump had remembered it. *Remembering* was not the problem; *forever* was.

The Christmas Classic went on for years after Bump's famous goal.

The photographs continued to fill the upstairs hallway of the old house, Bump growing until it seemed his own dad and the younger uncles were shrinking.

Younger players joined and older players fell off. Sometimes Bump would go up alone into the hallway and run a finger along the photographs. He was always careful not to touch and smear the glass. And he could silently name every player as he came to them — some of them in thirty or forty versions of their slowly changing faces.

The years since Bump posed for his very first Christmas Classic photograph had seemed to pass, on first glance, without much change — apart, of course, from Bump's own sprouting up.

But then Bump began to trace the changes. Faces dropping out. Two of the older Uncles retired.

Three photographs after Bump's first appearance on the wall of photos, there was no Grandpa Finnigan.

To Grandma's great relief, Grandpa had announced he was hanging up his skates . . . forever.

Change was taking place everywhere.

There had been a point at the Finnigan Christmas gatherings when many of the men smoked. Then there was a time when none of the men smoked and some of the young women smoked. Now no one smoked.

One year Uncle Jimmy failed to deliver his traditional hip check. The next year he was missing from the photograph, player and hip retired from action.

The Classic went on, though no one ever dared attempt to take up Uncle Jimmy's mantle of play-by-play broadcaster.

New and younger players joined in and played without Uncle Jimmy's famous initiation, though it was always spoken of over the Christmas meal — usually by Uncle Jimmy himself — as if the hip check was as much a beloved family tradition as Grandma's Talking Santa.

Bump's father, Wilf, took over the organizing of the national anthem, but no one could ever quite sang it with the off-key force and joy of Grandpa.

No matter. They sang it anyway, their voices loud enough that those waiting in the house and watching at the windows could hear.

And Bump still didn't know all the words.

Next year, he told himself. Next year.

Bump went through a stretch of four years when his name was engraved three different times onto the chrome hubcap as MVP of the Christmas Classic.

For the first two awards, it read "Bump Finnigan."

In the third, it became "Walt Finnigan."

Bump didn't win the trophy again, but he was now known by all as "Walt."

It wasn't so bad as he'd feared.

Walt became a better-than-average hockey player and won a scholarship to a university that eventually made him into a teacher. He married a lovely girl, Beverly, and they now had two children, a four-year-old boy, Jeremy, and a two-year-old girl, Lisa.

His grandpa had insisted, right from little Jeremy's first impossible steps, that the little guy be called "Bump." And now everyone called him "Bump" so automatically that "Jeremy," like "Walter" so many years before, had vanished from the family mouth.

Things were now changing so fast that Walt sometimes wondered how he could ever have once wished change could happen in the blink of an eye.

The old folks wanted to hold on to the farm for as long as they could, and no one in the Finnigan family ever suggested otherwise.

But then the Christmas came when there was no photograph of the Christmas Classic.

It had nothing to do with the Finnigans heading off for that once-in-a-lifetime trip to DisneyWorld.

It had nothing to do with family members having a falling out as so many families so foolishly do from time to time.

It had nothing to do with the weather.

In fact, the weather was ideal.

December 24, Christmas Eve, was bright and crisp when Denzil Finnigan woke and rubbed the fat of his hand along the bedroom window until the frost melted away and the new day took form.

"Going to be a beautiful day," Grandpa said back over his pajama shoulder to his wife, who was still in bed.

"How much fell?" Grandma asked.

He looked again, snow-white mustache rising in delight.

"Must be a foot."

He ploughed out the laneway with the tractor and then came back in for breakfast.

The kitchen was warm and filled with the smell of eggs and bacon. There was fresh coffee on. Toast popped just as he placed his winter coat on one rack and carefully set his cap on the one beside it.

"I'll eat and then shovel the rink off," he said.

"You leave that until some of the boys get here," Grandma said sharply, her back still to her husband as she flipped his eggs over once lightly.

He made no answer.

"Did you hear what I said?" she asked.

She turned around.

He had not heard what she said.

He was dead on the floor, his big heart seized as surely as a tractor engine that had run dry of oil.

They held the funeral the day after Boxing Day.

Walt and Annie — like "Bump," she had lost her "Poodle" — served as pallbearers with four of their cousins.

Walt sat in the front row of the service, holding tight to Annie's hand and trying to shake a thought that clung to his brain like a burr on a shoelace.

So much, he thought, for the guarantees of turkey gizzard.

So much for forever.

# MEMENTOS

They had one last Christmas at the old home. Grandma said she didn't like living there alone. She said her hips were giving her almost as much trouble as her memory and she wanted a place with no stairs. A small apartment in town would be better, she said, and no one argued with her even though they knew what it would mean for everyone else.

They played one final Christmas Classic on the pond. Uncle Jimmy, now into his seventies, came and stood on the banks and even, for old times' sake, shouted out a bit of play-by-play. He hadn't dressed but the players named Uncle Jimmy the MVP anyway and gave him the name-filled hubcap as a memento of his glory years on the frozen pond. It would be his to keep, forever.

Uncle Jimmy took the old hubcap and, for once, had nothing to say. His mouth quivered, but not a sound came out. No one asked him to repeat himself.

No one argued when the property was put up for sale. No one from town wanted to move out and take over the old farm. No one from the city wanted to move back. They could keep it for holidays but the upkeep would be expensive and, besides, as Uncle Donny said, a farm needs to be worked.

They held an auction to sell off the old farm equipment and the furniture. The family divided up what meant far too much to let go.

Walt, with everyone's blessing, moved the Christmas Classic portrait gallery out to the lake, where he lined the wall of the largest room of the old cabin with the framed photographs.

He took out the measuring door, and installed it at the cabin so that all still-growing and future Finnigans could keep up the tradition.

And there was one more thing he was given, though it had never occurred to him to ask for it.

"The Talking Santa should be yours, Walt," his sister Annie said as she came up the stairs from the cellar, dusting off the old Christmas ornament.

"Why me?"

She laughed. "Because no one worked harder to make him talk than you."

He took it happily. The Santa face was faded, the red looking faint and brittle, but the tongue was still there.

"Try it," Annie said.

Walt checked his thumb. His nails were sometimes still soft; he still chewed them when he was worried. He turned the tongue in his hand, pressed his nail hard to the serrated edge and yanked down hard.

*"Merrrrr—rrrrry Churrrisssssss-musssss!"*

It worked! He was looking down at Santa's tongue when he felt Annie's lips brush against his cheek in a quick kiss.

He looked at his sister but Annie was already turning away, her eyes glistening.

# ONE MORE TIME

A nnie and her family joined Walt's family at the cabin the first Christmas after the farm had gone.

The weather was perfect — crisp and cold, with the night laying down a fresh blanket of snow — and in the morning the telephone began ringing before breakfast.

Uncle Eric called from his place in Florida. Aunts called from the city and cousins from the coasts. Everyone wanted to wish each other a happy holiday and everyone, of course, had to mention how much they were going to miss the Christmas Classic.

When Uncle Jimmy called, he hung up before they could even say goodbye. Annie thought it must have been a lost connection. Walt agreed, but thought quietly to himself it had nothing to do with the telephone company. Walt thought he had heard Uncle Jimmy's voice starting to crack.

After lunch, with the sun shining down through the high pines, Walt decided to shovel off a small rink for the little ones.

He worked on late into the afternoon, his layers of clothes piled on the dock as he stripped down to a thin shirt for working.

"Use a hand?"

Walt looked up. He hadn't seen Annie's husband, Nate, come down through the drifts. Nate, who didn't even skate, had a shovel over his shoulder.

"Sure," Walt said.

They worked together, the rink spreading wider and wider across the bay until it was two, then three times what Walt had intended.

It had grown to the size of the rink on the old pond.

"You got any plywood?" Nate asked.

Walt remembered some stashed under the cabin. He nodded and they climbed the hill and hauled out two sheets, setting one up at each end to serve as both goals and endboards at the same time.

With darkness falling, they chopped a hole in the ice and drew enough water to flood the rink with pails. And in the evening, when the moon came out, the dark, fresh ice glistened yellow as they looked down from the main cabin window.

"We should play it," Nate said.

Walt turned, puzzled.

"The Christmas Classic," said Annie. "We should do it in honor of all those who can no longer play."

"You don't even skate," Walt said to Nate.

"I'll play in my boots. Those who can skate, skate. Those who can't, can still play. I'm game."

Walt shrugged: *why not?*

They all dressed to play. Nate and Annie and their two slightly older kids, Kelly and Jamie, Walt and Bev and even little Bump, with his own sawed-off stick and his boots.

They scrambled down the hill and out onto the black ice, the light from the cabin washing down over the snow and brightening the rink.

Walt sat on the end of the dock to put on his skates. He stepped out. It felt old, familiar, lovely. He stickhandled a puck for a while, reveling in the sound, delighting in the memories.

*"The anthem!"* Nate shouted out.

Walt stopped, turned and looked around. The others, little Bump included, were all standing in a perfect line, all at attention.

Walt skated over to join them, the sound of his skates filling the bay.

He stopped, stood sheepishly at attention, and Nate began singing.

*"O Canada . . . Our home and native land . . . "*

The kids knew the words best. Kelly and Jamie knew the French as well and bellowed the anthem out in both languages, Walt following along as best he could, at times mumbling in embarrassment.

*What a country*, he thought. *We know every word to Stompin' Tom's "The Hockey Song," but the only people who can sing the entire anthem are kids and professional anthem singers.* He still hadn't kept his promise to memorize every word of "O Canada."

They sang and then they played, a rough, uneven game that at times made little sense and at times seemed hopelessly unbalanced — Walt swooping about the ice effortlessly while Nate slid and slipped and tried to run in his boots — but it was still a game.

It had a score.

It had its moments, including a pretty fair Walt impression of Grandpa Finnigan's famous move when he dropped the puck back into his skates and turned poor Annie inside out as she tried to check her brother.

It wasn't the same but it was the same. The sounds of puck against board. The scraping sound of skate blades on natural ice. Even the icy air through wet nostrils felt the same to Walt.

He began skating faster and faster. It was, really, unfair to the other skaters and most assuredly unfair to poor Nate, who was hopeless in his big winter boots. But no one seemed bothered by Walt showing off. They seemed to want it.

He could feel his light jacket rippling as he turned sharply. He could feel his hair flying — even if there was no longer that much of it!

He looked in Annie's laughing face and saw Poodle.

He looked in his son's laughing face and saw . . . two Bumps.

His son.

And himself.

They played and, in the end, no one even bothered with scores or play-by-play. But they played, and when it was over they felt as if they had done something important, something necessary.

They had played the Christmas Classic.

*"HHHHELLPPPPPPPPPP!"*

It was Bump, and he was crying and screaming at the same time.

He had gone through the snowbank that Walt and Nate had built up around the rink.

He was down to his waist, terrified he was going right through to the bottom of the lake.

*"HHHHELLLLLLLLPPPPPPPPPPPPPPPPPP MEEEEE!"*

Walt skated over quickly, knowing there was no possibility whatsoever that the child could also break through a foot of hard ice.

He reached and pulled at Bump's arm, but the boy held fast.

Nate took the other arm and the two men pulled together — little Bump popping out like a carrot being pulled out of the garden.

*Minus one boot!*

Walt couldn't believe it.

They tried to retrieve the boot but it was lost in the darkness.

"Never mind," he told his son. "We'll get it tomorrow when we can see."

Or in the spring — just like his own so many years ago.

# FOREVER

**W**alt had trouble sleeping that night.

The adults had stayed up late, sipping coffee and talking about the game and about the glory of all the past Classics.

It wasn't the coffee that was keeping him awake.

And it wasn't the hardwood trees cracking like rifle shots in the bitter cold.

It was the wind, a wind picking up as it howled and hammered at the cabin to a point where, at times, it felt like the building was being picked up, shaken, and dropped back down.

Walt was glad he hadn't yet shoveled off the roof. The snow might keep the roof on.

Sometime during the night, he must have dozed off, for he woke to Bev's voice.

She was standing by the window, using the side of her hand to melt away the frost enough to look out.

"Come and look," she said.

Walt got up and went to the window.

*The lake had turned completely black!*

He looked again, rubbing the sleep out of his eyes.

"What is it?" he asked.

"The wind has blown the lake clear," she said. "It's solid ice."

Walt stared out, focusing.

The wind had died down, and as far as he could see down the bay, the ice was as shiny and black as the rink he and Nate had built the previous afternoon.

"You've got the world's largest rink now," Bev said, laughing.

"I'm going out," Walt said.

"What?"

"I'm going to skate it."

"You're crazy!" she giggled. She knew him too well to argue.

Walt dressed quickly and tiptoed out into the living room where he sat in a chair beside the old plastic Santa and began pulling on his winter boots.

"You're going out to skate, aren't you?"

He looked up. It was Annie, still bundled in her pajamas. She was smiling.

"Did you look out?" Walt asked his sister.

"I saw," she said. "It's like that day Grandpa used to talk about."

Walt nodded. He remembered their grandfather's story about the time it had rained for days and then the temperature had plummeted and everything had frozen. *Everything* — ponds, creeks, fields, roofs, cars, trees, the laneway, even the road into town.

Grandpa had told them how he and the Uncles had skated all the way to town and back. They had played shinny through every street and field and creek along the way. They had skated uphill and downhill. And they had arrived back at the farmhouse soaked and exhausted from what they called "The Longest Hockey Game Ever Played."

"Take Bump with you," Annie said.

Walt looked up. He hadn't thought of that.

Then he remembered the lost boot.

"He has no boots."

"Put Jamie's skates on him," she said.

"They're too big."

"Stuff them with socks — it's how everyone starts."

Walt could see the decision was already made for him. Annie was digging out Jamie's skates and searching through the packsacks for thick socks.

He tiptoed back to the children's bedroom where Bump was sleeping in one of the double beds, his sister in the other.

Careful not to wake the little girl, Walt leaned down and, without even thinking about it, rubbed his whiskered chin along the smooth cheek of his son. A small whisker burn to wake the child.

Bump's eyes flickered open.

"Hi Dad," he said, his voice still dripping with sleep.

"You want to skate the lake?" Walt whispered.

Bump scrunched his face, unsure.

"The rink covers the entire lake," Walt said. "Wanna skate it?"

"I don't have any skates."

"You can use your cousin's — Aunt Annie says."

The boy's eyes seemed to explode. Walt knew, in an instant, that the boy had been dreaming of this as much as he had once dreamed of playing in the Christmas Classic.

They bundled up as best they could, moving quickly and quietly.

Annie was waiting in the kitchen, four pairs of socks laid out. She worked them on and then pushed on Jamie's hockey skates and tied them.

The skates looked far too big, funny even — but neither Walt nor Annie dared laugh.

Walt carried his own skates in one arm and the heavily bundled Bump in the other. He worked his way down the hill to the end of the dock, where he sat to take off his boots and tie up his skates.

He could see more of the lake from here, and it was the most amazing sight he had ever seen.

This was better than the ice world Grandpa and the Uncles had skated over. The lake was flat, just like a rink. The ice was perfect, just as if the wind had been a Zamboni going back and forth all night long.

His skates on, he bent and picked up Bump.

He skated out onto the lake with Bump still hanging off his shoulder, the little boy's oversized skates dangling dangerously around Walt's upper leg.

Walt stopped skating and knelt on one knee.

He steadied Bump, the child slipping on the large skates and almost falling flat.

Walt caught him under the arms and, holding him upright while the little boy kicked helplessly, began skating out toward the island.

The wind was picking up again.

Walt rounded the far point and headed out into the breach of the lake, where the full force of the blow could be felt.

*"This is fun!"* Bump shouted, his voice instantly clipped off by the buffeting wind.

Walt turned them slightly, tucked his hands more firmly under the boy's arms and felt a gust stagger the two of them from the side.

He had no choice but to turn so his back was against the wind, the steady gusts now cupping in under Walt's arms and propelling him along — just as so many years ago Grandpa's big hands had swept him around the frozen pond of the Christmas Classic.

Then it blew even harder, catching him along his shoulders and back and propelling him hard ahead, almost as if he were once again the child and the wind the instructor.

And in a way it was.

Walt and Bump were no longer skating; they were *sailing*.